OTIS DOODA

DOWNRIGHT DANGEROUS

OTIS DOODA
DOWNRIGHT DANGEROUS

by ELLEN POTTER

ILLUSTRATIONS by DAVID HEATLEY

FEIWEL AND FRIENDS ◆ New York, NY

A Feiwel and Friends Book
An Imprint of Macmillan

Feiwel and Friends books may be purchased for business or promotional use.
For information on bulk purchases, please contact the Macmillan Corporate
and Premium Sales Department at (800) 221-7945 x5442 or by e-mail at
specialmarkets@macmillan.com

Library of Congress Cataloging-in-Publication Data Available

ISBN: 978-1-250-01177-0 (hardcover) / 978-1-250-01179-4 (ebook)

Book design by Véronique Lefèvre Sweet and David Heatley

Feiwel and Friends logo designed by Filomena Tuosto

First Edition: 2014

1 3 5 7 9 10 8 6 4 2

mackids.com

For Ian, Clay, Louisa, Maya, and Sam

TABLE OF CONTENTS

This Is 100% Not a Lie   1

Digging in the Treasure Box   3

Big Chunks   8

The Greatest Lego Genius Who Ever Lived   15

Devil Dog   20

Bubble Blasters   26

Belly Button Poppers   38

Jaws of Death   50

Hee-Hee-Hee   59

Bob the Goldfish   64

Free Advice   73

Boris Saliva   74

Otis Dooda, Crocodile Wrestler   82

Lethal Lunch   86

I'm a Li'l Stinker   93

Invisibility Vests   100

Swamp Gas   105

Diabolical   117

Alien Eggs   123

Bzzzzzz!   129

Agent Shaw   136

Alien Baby Invasion   143

Nostril Tricks   154

Face-Holes   160

Mighty Mack 500   163

My Disgusting Family   170

2 Weird 4 Gunther   174

Robot Yellow Jackets   179

The Anti-Alien Patrol   188

War of the Worlds   195

Giant Bummer   206

Dingle-Dork of the Week   213

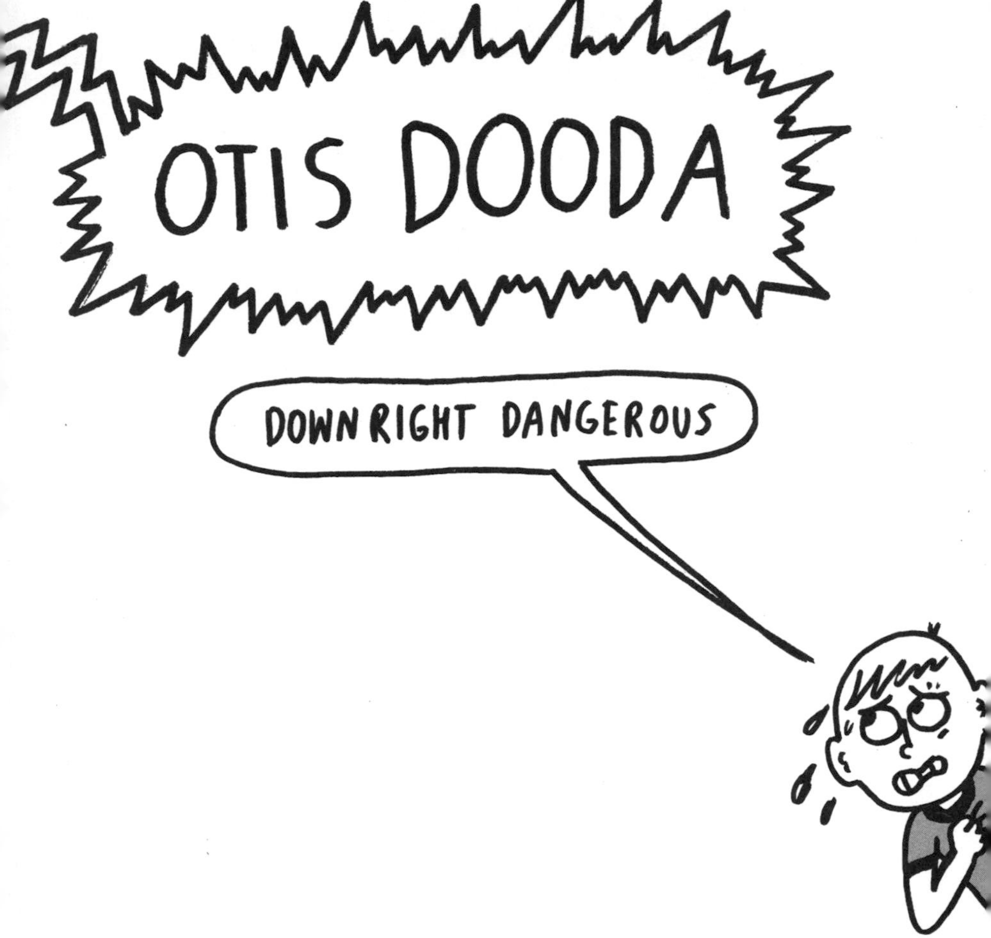
OTIS DOODA
DOWNRIGHT DANGEROUS

THIS IS 100% (NOT) A LIE

One thing you should know about me is that I don't lie. Not very much, anyway. I don't have anything against lying. It's just that I'm bad at it. Whenever I tell a lie, I sweat like a pig in a bacon factory. Plus, I start talking like an eighty-year-old man.

The reason I'm telling you this is because you are probably going to think this book is made up. It's not. It's all 100% true. The thing is, some weird stuff has happened to me since I moved to New York City this past summer. You might have heard about some of it.

But now there's more.

DIGGING IN THE

If there's one thing I can't stand, it's the morning of the first day of school. You wake up all tired and wobbly because you've been staying up late the whole summer. Then you have to go to the bathroom and brush things that you haven't brushed for a while and get dressed before you've even watched any TV.

It's unnatural.

That morning, my older brother, Gunther, and I sat slumped at the

kitchen table, looking miserable while shoveling cereal into our mouths.

Mom was in a great mood, though.

"Aren't you guys excited?" she said. "A new school in *New York City!*"

"No," we both said at the same time.

But *she* sure was excited. You know why? Because she was finally going to get rid of us for a few hours. I know that's true because I saw it in her text message to Dad. Mom and Dad text-message when they want to tell each other things they don't want us to hear. Then later, when Mom goes to the bathroom, I look at her cell phone and see what's really going on.

4

Gunther looked at me over his cereal bowl with this cheesy smile on his face.

"You know what happens to new kids, don't you?" he said.

"What?" I said. I knew I shouldn't ask, but I couldn't help myself. I'd never actually been the new kid at a school before.

"The only person who'll sit next to you is the kid who digs in the treasure box," Gunther said.

"What does that mean?"

"Digging . . . in . . . the . . . treasure . . . box." Gunther demonstrated by pretending to pick his nose.

The funny thing is, I have never seen Gunther *actually* pick his nose. Since he's a pretty

disgusting guy in general, this always seemed strange to me. I once asked Mom about it.

"Maybe it's because he has good manners," she said.

But we both knew that was ridiculous. So she gave me a stern look and said, "Let's not talk about it, okay? It's very upsetting to Gunther."

That's why I like to bring it up every once in a while.

"Hey, that reminds me, Gunther," I said, "why don't you pick your nose? Are you afraid of the boogeyman?"

Gunther threw a Cheerio at me and hit me right in the eyeball. I flicked a spoon of milk at his head. Mom walked back in, took one look at us, and started text-messaging Dad like mad.

BIG CHUNKS

I hate to admit it, but Gunther was right!

The lady at the school's main office told me to go to Room 214. I was one of the first people there, so I grabbed a two-seater desk in the back of the room. I like to be as invisible as possible in class.

A few minutes later all these kids come pouring into the classroom. Nobody sat next to me. I even smiled at a couple of them to encourage them. I

got the Stink Eye from those kids. After a while I gave up and just read the stuff that people had written on the desks. Let me tell you, some of it was pretty bad. Parents are always so worried about what kids watch on TV. But if they knew what was written on the classroom desks, they'd never let their kids step inside a school.

I made a mental note to try this argument out on Mom.

Suddenly I heard the chair next to me scrape against the floor and I looked over to see—

You'll never guess.

I'll give you a hint.

He's the most annoying person on the planet. Not counting Gunther.

That's right. Boris! Boris who lives on the fourth floor of my apartment building! I couldn't believe he was in the third grade. He practically looks like a grown man. Seriously, you could carpet a bedroom with all his leg hair.

"Well, if it isn't Thinny McSkelebones!" Boris said as he sat down next to me.

"Hi, Boris," I muttered.

"Lucky for you I'm in your class, huh?" he said. "I heard Mrs. West is really strict, so don't be too chummy with me or she'll separate us."

"Good to know," I said.

If I had to kiss Boris in order to get Mrs. West to move me, I would.

Just then Cat walked in. She lives on the same floor as I do in Tidwell Towers. She spotted us right away and walked to the back of the room. There were two girls sitting at the desk next to ours, but Cat pointed at one of them and said, "Take a hike, sister." And you know what? The girl did.

Cat weighs about as much as a paper bag, but she's very scary.

"Good news," Cat said to us. "Mrs. West was attacked by a duck over the summer and she broke her hip. We're going to have a new teacher."

"Yes!" Boris pounded his fists on the desk. I snorted. "A duck? Really?"

"Don't laugh, man," Boris said, his eyes wide. "Ducks are the most dangerous form of poultry."

Suddenly, the whole class got quiet. A man had walked into the room. He was a young guy

with longish brown hair and he was wearing round glasses.

"Hey, Room 214, what's sizzling? I'm your new teacher this year. My name is Mr. Koslowski. But because I like you, you can call me Mr. K."

Boris's hand shot up in the air.

"Yes?" Mr. K said to Boris.

"You can call me Big Chunks," Boris told him.

"Will do, Big Chunks," Mr. K said.

I couldn't believe what a sucker this guy was! Boris's hand shot up again.

"Yes, Big Chunks?" Mr. K said.

"You can call him Little Chunks," Boris said, pointing to me.

I started shaking my head and mouthing, *No, no!*

"Hmm." Mr. K looked at me and tipped his head to one side. "He looks more like a Captain Mayhem to me."

"I think I like this guy," I whispered to Boris. But he wasn't paying attention.

He was too busy digging in his treasure box.

THE GREATEST LEGO GENIUS WHO EVER LIVED

At recess there were three different games of tag going on. Boris insisted I play this game called Killer Octopus Tag. I think Boris made the game up, because it was totally ridiculous. The person who was It had to walk around the playground in slow motion with their arms waving, saying, UHHHHHH, UHHHHH... while everyone else ran away.

"Otis is It!" Boris called.

But every time I started to run, Boris yelled, "Octopuses can't run!"

It got boring really quickly, so I quit and I walked off to find another game. A bunch of girls were playing Pony Tag, where they all had to gallop around, shake their heads, and make snorting noises. That didn't seem too great, either. The other tag game was Ninja Tag. Cat was playing that one. As far as I could tell, the object of Ninja Tag was to kick as many people as you could.

But I'm not really the violent type.

I'm more like the sissy type.

Plus, when I kick I look like a stork that's being electrocuted.

Instead, I just went on the monkey bars and hung upside down. I love hanging upside down. I could do it for hours.

I was just hanging there, watching this kid named Trevor McBride lick a smooshed Starburst on the bottom of his sneaker. Suddenly, this other boy walked up to me. He had the biggest ears I've ever seen. It looked like he had two bagels glued to the sides of his head.

"You're the Lego nerd," he said.

"Who told you that?" I asked him.

The kid shrugged. "I hear things."

With ears like that, I bet you do, I thought.

I didn't say it out loud though. I don't like it when people make fun of my skinniness. So I just made fun of him in my head.

"If you know what's good for you, don't mess with Sid Frackas," the kid said.

"Who's Sid Frackas?" I asked.

The kid stuck one finger in the air and said, "He's the greatest Lego genius who ever lived!"

I looked at him for a moment. Then I asked, "By any chance, are you Sid Frackas?"

The kid frowned at me. "Maybe I am and maybe I ain't." Then he started to walk away.

"Okay, bye, Sid Frackas!" I called after him.

He didn't answer.

"Nice chatting with you, Sid old boy!" I called.

His ears turned very red.

The recess bell rang and on the way back into the classroom, Cat said, "Why were you talking to Sid Frackas?"

"You know him?" I asked.

"Sure," she said. "He lives in our building. Also he's the greatest Lego genius who ever lived."

"Oh." I wasn't too thrilled about that.

Because I always thought I was the greatest Lego genius who ever lived.

DEVIL DOG

On the way home Mom asked me the same old question she always asks.

"So what did you do at school?"

"I don't remember," I told her.

The thing is, after I'm finished with school, all my memories of the day leak out of my brain. I honestly can't remember a single thing that happened. Like people who have been in a traumatic accident.

Mom was walking this Boston terrier named Diablo, which is Spanish for "devil." Let me tell you, that dog lived up to his name. His owners enrolled him in Mom's dog school, Horrible Hounds Academy, because he tries to bite anything that comes near his mouth. And you know what my mom does? She bites him back.

No kidding. She flips him over and bites his throat.

While growling.

In public.

We had to stop about twelve times on the way home so Mom could bite Diablo.

When she wasn't biting Diablo, though, she kept grilling me about what I did in school.

Finally, I said to her, "What did YOU do all day?"

She got all guilty looking and said,

I DON'T REMEMBER.

When we went into the lobby of our apartment building, I fished around in my pocket, then pulled out a stick of gum and tossed it into a jack-o'-lantern bucket sitting by a potted plant. I could see Potted Plant Guy staring out at me from behind the leaves. He's this kid who sits in a potted plant in the lobby. If you don't put something in Potted Plant Guy's pail when you walk into the building, he puts a curse on you.

Seriously, you don't want to mess with that crazy kid.

My mom tossed a fruit roll into his pail. She doesn't actually believe the curse thing. She just does it because she thinks he's adorable.

He's about as adorable as a sharp stick in your eye.

We took the elevator up to the thirty-fifth floor. We live on the very top floor of Tidwell Towers, which is pretty cool. But my favorite thing about it is that my best friend, Perry Hooper, lives on the thirty-fifth floor, too.

When we got off the elevator, I spotted a big cardboard box right outside Perry's apartment door. Knowing the Hoopers, there was something interesting in it. And possibly dangerous.

So of course I had to go investigate.

"Mom, can I go to the Hoopers'?" I asked.

At that moment the elevator door opened and the old lady who lives next door to us stepped out. Diablo made a lunge for her, and Mom answered me while she was biting Diablo, so it came out sounding like

WIFFNOD POTZ.

Which I just assumed was yes.

BUBBLE BLASTERS

"Hey, Otis," Mr. Hooper said as he opened the door. When he saw the big box, he clapped his hands.

"Woo-hoo!! It came! Perry, it came!!" he cried.

We lugged the box inside. It was really heavy and whatever was inside was clattering around.

Perry swatted me on the back to say hi. And guess who else was there?

That's right.

Boris.

He was sprawled out on their couch, eating a pickle smeared with cream cheese. He eats disgusting stuff like that. But if you say it's disgusting or make a face, he gets all upset and says you are making fun of his family's heritage, even though no one has any idea what his family heritage is. So I tried not to look at the pickle with cream cheese as we opened the box.

Inside the first box there was another box. Someone had written BOY STUFF on top of it. Mr. Hooper smiled and rubbed his hands together.

"What is it?" I asked.

"Something for The Big Green Party Machine," Perry said.

That's Mr. Hooper's green school bus. He fills it with games and things, then

brings it to kids' birthday parties. Only his games are always pretty cruddy. Or busted. Or lethal.

"I have a big party coming up," Mr. Hooper said. "Thirty boys are going to be there. I saw this box of Boy Stuff online and thought it would be perfect."

Then we opened the box marked BOY STUFF. There were plastic swords, bows and arrows with water balloons for tips, something called a

Toilet Paper Launcher, and a whole lot of other things that I couldn't identify.

Mr. Hooper pulled out a plastic baggie full of little green buttons. He took out a piece of paper from inside the baggie, read it, and smiled.

"What are they?" I asked.

"Belly Button Poppers."

"Cool! Let's try them!" Perry said.

I wasn't so sure. Putting a popper in my belly button sounded like a bad idea. Plus, I'm sort of sensitive about my belly button because it's really deep. Gunther used to stuff frozen peas in it when I was younger.

Mr. Hooper read the instructions: " 'Peel off sticky back. Insert Belly Button Popper in belly button. In one to two minutes, you will feel it begin to vibrate. Lift up your shirt. The Belly Button Popper will shoot out of your belly button.' "

Perry took one of the Belly Button Poppers, peeled off the back, lifted his shirt up, and stuck

the popper in his belly button. We all stared at his belly button for one to two minutes.

Nothing happened.

Boris tried it, too. His belly button was so hairy that he had a hard time sticking the green thing into it.

Yecch.

We waited a few minutes, but nothing happened to his popper, either.

"I guess they don't work," I said, relieved.

"Or maybe our belly buttons are no good. Let's try yours."

So I had to stick that thing in my belly button, and everyone stared at it while we waited for the popper to shoot out. I kept expecting Boris to say something about my weird belly button, but I guess when your own belly button is full of hair, everyone else's seems pretty normal.

Anyway, nothing happened.

"They're probably heat activated," Mr. Hooper said. "Try leaving them in and see what happens."

That didn't thrill me, but Perry, Boris, and I

left them in while we all looked through the box and pulled out some water guns.

Only they weren't actual water guns.

"They're *Bubble* Blasters," Mr. Hooper said excitedly.

Perry, Boris, and I groaned.

"Soap bubbles, Dad? Really?" Perry said. "That's kind of lame."

"Not soap bubbles," Mr. Hooper said. "Gum bubbles."

He examined the instructions taped to one of the Bubble Blasters.

"'First,'" he read, "'put on protective Bubble Blaster jacket.'" He shrugged his shoulders. "That seems silly. Let's skip that part."

Uh-oh, I thought.

Then he tossed us each a block of gum the size of a cell phone.

"Start chewing, boys!" he said.

My gum tasted like banana. Weird, but not bad. We all chewed and chewed and chewed until our mouths were stuffed full of giant slimy balls.

"Okay," Mr. Hooper said, handing us each a blaster. "Load 'em up."

I crammed the gum into this hole in the back of the blaster. Boris was examining his gum, which had bits of green and white things in it.

"Wow, what flavor did you have?" I asked.

"Oh, that's just the pickle and cream cheese from between my teeth," he said.

Yecch, again.

"Now, when you press the button, the Bubble Blaster will blow a bubble," Mr. Hooper said.

Frankly, it seemed like a lot of work for nothing. Our jaws were hurting and our fingers were all spitty from loading the blaster.

The doorbell rang.

"Go on, boys," Mr. Hooper said as he went to open the door. "Let's see how these babies work."

Perry and I each pushed the button and . . . WOW!

Instead of blowing bubbles, the chewed-up gum shot out of the blaster like a cannonball. Perry's piece knocked over a coffee cup and a lamp, and landed *SPLAT!* against the window.

My piece flew clear across the room, through the door that Mr. Hooper had just opened, and landed *SPLAT!* on Cat's glasses.

I know it was rude, but she looked so funny with that big blob of gum on her glasses I started laughing. That's when Boris decided to shoot his bubble gum right into my mouth.

For the record, pickles with cream cheese tastes just as revolting as it sounds.

BELLY BUTT☼N P☼PPERS

As it turned out, Cat is pretty touchy about things getting stuck to her glasses. For a second it looked like she was going to brain me. But then I showed her Boris's revolting gum and told her that it had landed in my mouth, and she cheered right up.

Mr. Hooper wasn't so happy, though. "Bummer! Looks like this box is full of duds." Then he took Cat's glasses in the kitchen to scrape off the gum for her.

We all stared at Cat. Without her glasses she looked like Master Shifu from *Kung Fu Panda*.

"What are you looking at?" she asked us.

Perry and I had enough sense to keep our mouths shut, but of course Boris didn't.

"You know who you look like without your glasses?" Boris said.

"Who?" Cat said.

Perry and I looked around the room for something to hide behind.

"You look like my cousin, Brenda," Boris said.

We breathed a sigh of relief.

"And a little like Master Shifu from *Kung Fu Panda*," Boris added.

We waited for things to start flying. But Cat just rolled her eyes and said, "*Any*way. I have good news, guys. I found the perfect old guy for our homework."

"What homework?" I asked.

Like I said, once I leave school all memory of what happened inside those walls is completely erased.

"Our homework to interview an old person about their career. Sheesh!" Cat said. "Mr. K said that we could interview someone as a group, so I thought we could all go talk to Mr. Rollo on the fourteenth floor."

The thought of sitting in some old guy's house while he clipped his yellow toenails gave me the jim-jams. Which is worse than the heebie-jeebies.

Cat must have seen my expression because she added, "Mr. Rollo used to be a New York City police officer."

Well, that sounded better. If you have to watch an old guy clip his toenails, there might as well be a few car chases and bank robberies thrown in.

Even Perry wanted to come along, and he didn't even have ANY homework. His dad homeschools him.

I once suggested to Mom that she homeschool me.

Her reply was, "How do you expect me to teach you long division when it took me five years to teach you not to pee in the pool?"

❊   ❊   ❊

When Mr. Rollo opened the door, I was glad to see that he wasn't too crusty. And he kept his shoes on the whole time we interviewed him, which was a big relief, toenail-wise.

It turned out that Mr. Rollo had been a cop for only one day.

That was disappointing. But on the positive side, there was this big bank robbery on that one day and Mr. Rollo was right in the middle of it.

"Those robbers came running out of the bank, shooting their pistols. Bullets were flying all over the place! One flew right by my left ear. Another flew over my head. I tell you, I've never been so scared in my life. I quit the police force that day. I still have nightmares about the whole thing."

Mr. Rollo looked all shook up just telling us the story.

"So that's why I became a ladies' shoe salesman," he said.

Then he started telling us all about ladies' feet. No kidding. He told us about different sorts of lumps on ladies' feet, and a woman with feet the size of a loaf of bread and another woman who had a miniature foot growing right on top of her big toe. It was all so disgusting that I started to get this weird feeling in my belly. I looked over at Perry. He looked like he was feeling the same way. Even Boris had this strange expression on his face.

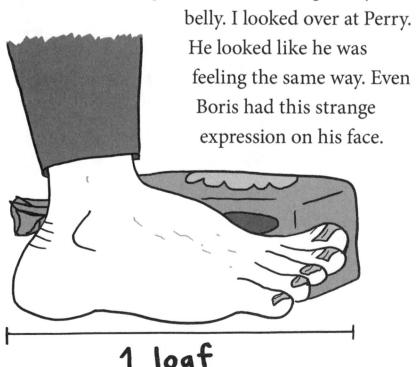

1 loaf

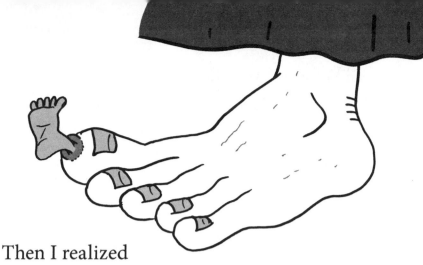

Then I realized
that it wasn't ladies' feet
that were making me feel funny.

It was the Belly Button Popper. The thing
was starting to vibrate in my belly button.

I glanced over at Perry. He looked back at
me, his eyes wide. Then he pointed at his belly.

I know, I mouthed.

"Dudes!" Boris shouted. "I'm vibrating!" He
yanked up his shirt. I thought he was just being
dramatic, until I saw Perry yank up his shirt,
also. Then I remembered. That's what you were
supposed to do when the Belly Button Popper
started to vibrate. So I yanked up my shirt, too.

"What are you doing!?" Cat shrieked at us.

Mr. Rollo just looked confused.

Perry's Belly Button Popper went off first. It started with a loud *tsssssss* sound, then a *BANG!* And it shot straight out of his belly button and flew right over Mr. Rollo's head, leaving behind a trail of smoke.

My popper shot out next. Maybe because my belly button is so deep, my popper had a

little extra oomph. *Tsssss . . . ba-ba-BA-BANG!!*
It zoomed right by Mr. Rollo's left ear. He
screamed and covered his head with his arms.

"Cut that out!" Cat demanded.

But it was too late. Boris's popper started the
tsssss noise and then it burst out of his belly
button. *BANG!* It didn't shoot straight out like

ours did. His flew high up in the air, almost to the ceiling. Then it started to plunge back down, with smoke trailing behind it. The really awful thing was that it was headed directly for Mr. Rollo. And the really, *really* awful thing was that it was covered in Boris's belly-button hair.

"Hit the deck, Mr. Rollo!" Cat yelled.

But Mr. Rollo was such a wreck that he just froze. It must have brought back all those memories of his day as a police officer. So Cat

launched herself out of her seat and caught the hairy popper while it was in midair. It was pretty impressive. Mostly because she actually touched the thing.

POP

POP

After that, Mr. Rollo had to go lie down on the couch with a cold washcloth over his face.

JAWS OF DEATH

Out in the hallway of the fourteenth floor we noticed that a brand-new *Tidwell Tidbits* had just been posted above the elevator buttons. The *Tidwell Tidbits* is a newsletter about things that go on in our building. It's written by this lady named Miss Yabby, who probably has nothing better to do.

TIDWELL TIDBITS Jr.

SPECIAL KIDS' ISSUE
CONTESTS, PRIZES & NEWS

If you see Deedee Spitz in the elevator, do NOT be alarmed by that huge purple thing on her forehead. It is not contagious. It's only a pimple. Don't stare at it and for heaven's sakes DO NOT mention it to other people. Deedee is very embarrassed by it and

would hate for the entire building to know about it.

Happy ninth birthday to Trevor McBride! Isn't he adorable? He must have stepped in something yummy!

What is Lego-genius Sid Frackas in apartment 29G working on now? Rumor has it, this thing is top secret! The first person to spill the beans about it to Miss Yabby will get twenty bucks. (Please see Julius to collect your reward .)

Miss Yabby

So of course we headed straight to 29G.

There was a group of kids already gathered outside the Frackas apartment. They did not look happy. A few of them were slumped against the wall and others were sitting on the floor.

"Forget about it," one boy told us. "Mrs. Frackas won't let anybody in."

I figured that would be the end of that. But Perry just marched right up to apartment 29G and rang the doorbell.

"Go away!" a lady inside yelled back.

"It's Perry Hooper, Mrs. Frackas," Perry said.

You wouldn't believe it, but the door opened right away. Grown-ups just love Perry, no

kidding. I mean he does the same bad stuff that we do, but grown-ups don't seem to notice.

The other kids tried to sneak into the apartment behind us, but Mrs. Frackas slapped them back with a flyswatter.

Sid's room was at the end of the hall. You could tell it was Sid's room right away because there was this big sign taped to the door:

KEEP OUT!
Signed,
The Greatest Lego
Genius Who Ever Lived

So of course we just walked right in.

What we saw made us all go, "Whoa!" The entire room was filled with a giant shark's head made out of Legos. There was a desk inside the shark's head that was covered with Legos, and sitting at that desk was Sid Frackas.

"Don't come any closer!" he shrieked. His hand was hovering over a metal box on his desk with a big red button. "When I press this button, the shark's jaws will snap shut and its razor-sharp teeth will slice you all to pieces!"

Then he pressed the red button. The shark's mouth really did begin to close. The only thing was, it closed so slowly that we just stepped right over the teeth and into the mouth, no problem. It took a few more minutes for the jaws to close all the way.

"You're lucky. You made it just in the nick of time," Sid said.

It was pitch-dark in there, so he didn't see us all roll our eyeballs.

"What are you working on, Sid?" Perry asked.

"Why should I tell *you*?" Sid replied.

"Because Miss Yabby is going to give us twenty bucks if we find out," Perry said.

"Ha! Twenty bucks?" Sid snorted. "That's peanuts compared to the five hundred dollars I'm going to get if I win the Crazy Vehicle Lego Contest."

Then Sid said, "Oops."

"Thanks for the tip, Sid!" Perry said happily. "We'll be on our way."

But Sid didn't open the shark's mouth.

"Come on, Sid, pop the lid already!" Cat said. "It smells like asparagus in here."

"No can do," Sid replied. "Now that you've found out my top-secret project, I can't let you leave. These Lego bricks are superglued together. You'll never see the light of day again!"

HEE-HEE-HEE

Being locked inside Sid's room really freaked me out because I'm afraid of the dark. It's because of something that happened back when we used to live in Hog's Head. For a whole month, I kept hearing noises in my room at night. *SLUUUUURP! SLURPITTY-SLURP . . . SLUUUUURP!* When I told my parents about it, they said it was just our old house creaking. But then one morning Mom went to get something from my closet and she found Grandma Loretta sleeping in there, surrounded by a bunch of empty strawberry Frosty shakes. It turns out she was escaping from the nursing home at night to drink strawberry Frostys in my closet. Since then

I've had a phobia about dark rooms. And I'm not too crazy about strawberry Frostys, either.

Now, in Sid's pitch-black room, my heart was pounding like crazy. I got all sweaty and started breathing so fast that I was making this hee-hee-hee sound.

"Who's laughing like that?" Sid demanded. "Is that you, Perry?"

"No," Perry said.

I was embarrassed to say it was my scaredy-cat breathing so I didn't say anything. I just kept going, "Hee-hee-hee."

"Well, quit it, whoever it is!" Sid said. "You're creeping me out!"

I was getting really frantic now. Then I remembered that red button on Sid's desk. I stuck my hands straight out in the darkness and started feeling around. After a minute or so, I smacked into something hard. The desk! Perfect!

I jabbed my finger into the blackness, poking at things until I finally felt something big and round. I stabbed my finger into it.

"HEY!!!" Sid screamed. "Who just stuck their finger in my ear??!!"

That's when someone farted.

"You know what?" Sid said. "You guys are disgusting! Get out of here!" He must have pressed the button because the shark's mouth started opening very slowly.

We ran out of there, and didn't stop running until we got to the elevator. Out in the hallway, Perry gave me a high-five.

"That creepy laugh was awesome," he said.

"Right?" I replied.

As you can see, I am not above taking credit for things that I really shouldn't.

Still, I *do* like to be fair. So I added, "But it was Boris's colossal fart that really did the trick."

"That wasn't my fart," Boris said.

"Well, it wasn't mine, either," said Perry.

We all looked at Cat. She smiled back.

That girl is full of surprises.

BOB the GOLDFISH

After we collected our twenty bucks from
Julius, we had Mr. Hooper give us change for it.
We each got $5.00. I now had $25.00 in my

piggy bank, since Grandma Loretta had sent me
a twenty-dollar bill for my birthday a while
back. Well, really Grandma Loretta sent me a
squished bug in an envelope. That's what she
sends Gunther and me every birthday. I think
it's because she thinks boys like bugs. Which I
do. Only I suspect she mails the bugs alive and
they get squished on the way. This year it was a
squished earwig. But Mom always throws the

bug in the garbage and gives us a twenty instead.

I went back home. The second I walked into my apartment, I knew something was wrong. It was because Gunther was sitting on the living room couch, looking happy. That was just weird. I narrowed my eyes at him.

"Okay," I said, "did you fill my socks with mayonnaise again?"

"Nope."

"Then why do you look so happy?" I asked.

"Because Pandora is coming to visit this weekend," he said.

I groaned. Pandora is only slightly better than putting your foot in a sock full of mayonnaise. She's Gunther's girlfriend, which right away tells you that there is something massively wrong with her. She still lives in Hog's Head. One of the many strange things about Pandora is that she's always scratching at her scalp. Maybe she's raising a colony of ants on her head.

"Well, she's not sleeping in my room," I said, imagining that scabby scalp on my bed.

Mom wasn't home. I guessed she was down at Diablo's apartment, talking to his owners about his "raisins." She says that Diablo's problem is that he still has his raisins. She says he needs to go to a vet and have them removed.

I didn't know what she meant at first. Gunther explained it to me, and HOLY NACHOS, that was disturbing!

Honestly, I don't think Mom should be going around telling people whose raisins need to be removed.

Anyway, I took Mom's laptop into my bedroom. I'm only allowed to use it for homework, so I booted it up and wrote the first line of my report:

Meet Mr. Rollo, hero cop and admirer of women's feet!

I knew he wasn't exactly a hero cop, but I felt

bad about scaring him with our Belly Button Poppers.

After that I Googled "Crazy Vehicle Lego Contest." There it was! Build a motorized Lego vehicle. First prize was $500.

I could do a lot with $500.

Like buy more Lego sets.

You had to bring your Lego entry to the Livingstone Museum of Science in Manhattan that upcoming Saturday. That didn't leave me much time, so I started thinking up ideas right away.

I considered a helicopter with a dragon head on it. Or a dune buggy that could do backflips. All of a sudden, though, I knew exactly what to build. A hovercraft! One that would really fly. I took out my sketchbook and started to draw up the design.

Suddenly I got the feeling that I was being watched. That's been happening a lot lately.

"Okay," I said. "Where are you?"

I checked under my desk. I looked in my toy basket. I checked the garbage can, and looked under my dresser.

Nothing.

Grrr.

It was when I sat down on my bed that I saw him. He was squatting on my pillow, staring at me with that spooky, blank expression.

"All right, Smoochie, scram!" I told him.

But he just kept staring at me.

In case you don't know, Smoochie is Gunther's pet rat.

This summer Smoochie fell off our thirty-fifth-floor terrace and parachuted down in a

Fritos bag. Which may have been my fault, but that's beside the point. Anyway, ever since then he keeps sneaking into my room and staring at me. It might be because he's brain damaged from the fall. Or he might just be trying to freak me out for revenge.

"Okay, Smoochie, you asked for it," I told him.

I went to my bookshelf and took down my secret anti-Smoochie weapon. His name is Bob the goldfish. I bought him off a girl on the third floor a few weeks ago. Smoochie is terrified of him, no kidding. I held Bob's bowl up to Smoochie's face. That's all it took. Smoochie squealed, jumped in the air, and shot out of the room.

My theory is that when Smoochie sees Bob the goldfish it gives him a flashback of when he used to live in a pet store and no one wanted to buy him. Sort of like Mr. Rollo's flashback when our Belly Button Poppers went off, only in rat version.

Which made me wonder if one day something really bad would happen to *me*, and I would get flashbacks, too.

FREE ADVICE

This isn't really a chapter. It's just a helpful tip: You should never wonder stuff like I just wondered in the last paragraph, because it's practically a guarantee that bad things will happen. Which they did.

BORIS SALIVA

In school the next day a nurse came into our classroom to talk to us about good hygiene.

"But we learned that stuff in kindergarten," said Trevor McBride.

"It won't hurt to refresh your memory," the nurse said, giving him a hard look.

I'm guessing she heard about Trevor eating the Starburst off the bottom of his sneaker.

First she asked us who uses hand sanitizers. A bunch of kids raised their hands, including me. I don't actually use hand sanitizer, but I didn't want people to think I was unsanitary.

Boris looked at me, horrified. "What do you use that gunk for?" he asked.

"To clean my hands, what do you think?" I said.

"You don't need hand sanitizer to clean your hands," he said. "Just lick them." He actually licked his hands till they were all slimy. "Human saliva has special cleaning germs in it."

"That's *dog* saliva," I said.

He snorted and smiled while shaking his head. "Where do you hear this crazy stuff, man?"

"Okay, class. Look at your hands," the nurse continued. "Do they look clean?"

"Yes!" we all said.

"Well, they may not be as clean as they look."

That sounded pretty menacing. The nurse pulled this gel out of her bag. She went around the room squirting it on our hands, then told us to rub it in. After that, she went up to one of the boys in the front of the class and shined this

little flashlight on his hands. His hands turned blue and had loads of glowing white splotches on them.

"Those white splotches are bacteria," the nurse told us.

We all made barfing noises.
I mean, I sort of felt sorry for the
kid, but honestly, it looked like he had just
been splashing around in the boys' toilet.

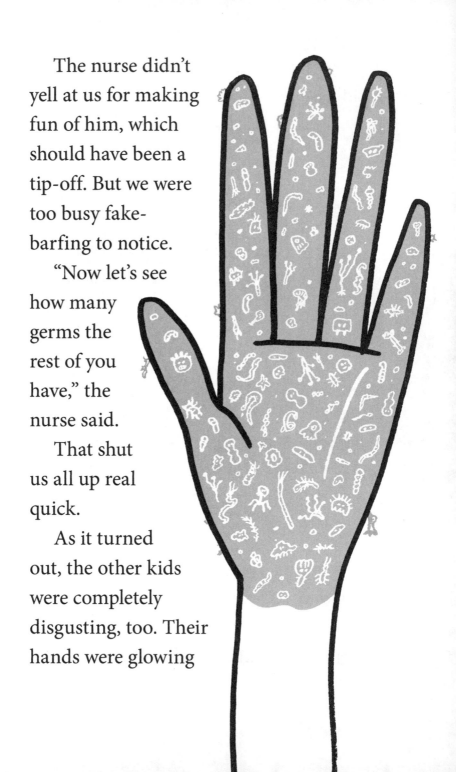

The nurse didn't yell at us for making fun of him, which should have been a tip-off. But we were too busy fake-barfing to notice.

"Now let's see how many germs the rest of you have," the nurse said.

That shut us all up real quick.

As it turned out, the other kids were completely disgusting, too. Their hands were glowing

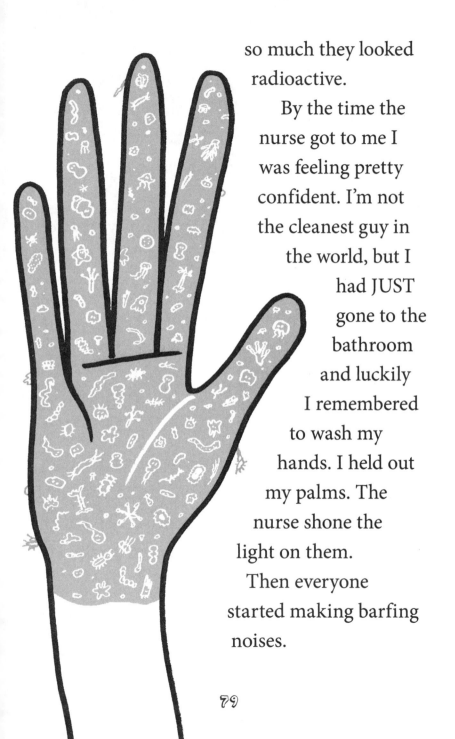

so much they looked radioactive.

By the time the nurse got to me I was feeling pretty confident. I'm not the cleanest guy in the world, but I had JUST gone to the bathroom and luckily I remembered to wash my hands. I held out my palms. The nurse shone the light on them. Then everyone started making barfing noises.

Because guess what? My perfectly clean hands had a billion glowing spots on them.

"This is such a SCAM!" I yelled. "My hands are squeaky clean!! This is just a trick to embarrass us!! Don't you nurses have something better to do than humiliate kids?"

The nurse did not look very happy with me.

"Settle down, Captain Mayhem," Mr. K said.

I may have overreacted. But I don't always remember to wash my hands after I go to the bathroom, and I think I should at least get credit for it when I do.

After that, the nurse shined her flashlight on Boris's hands.

You won't believe this, but there wasn't a single glowing spot on either of his hands. Not one. Even the nurse looked surprised. She held the light closer to his hands, then farther away.

No spots.

"Hmm. Those are the cleanest hands I've ever seen," she said.

"I licked them clean," Boris said proudly.

She laughed because she thought he was kidding.

After the nurse finished grossing us all out, she showed us how to wash our hands properly.

Then she said we shouldn't eat things that were stuck to the bottoms of our shoes.

OTIS DOODA,
CROCODILE WRESTLER

After the nurse left, Mr. K told us that this week we were going to learn about different jobs.

"Who knows what they want to be when they grow up?" he asked.

Cat raised her hand. "A bounty hunter."

"Not surprising. Anybody else?"

One kid wanted to be a veterinarian. Another kid named Jeffers said he wanted to be a sound-effects guy for movies. He said he already figured out how they make a sound effect in *Star Wars*.

"If you hold one end of a Slinky up to your ear and wiggle the other end, it sounds just like a *Star Wars* blaster," he said.

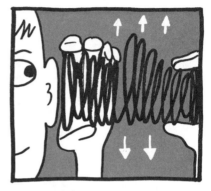

Try it. This actually works.

This girl named Myra said she wanted to either drive the truck that picks up roadkill or open her own burrito stand.

Note to future self: Never buy a burrito from anyone named Myra.

I didn't raise my hand. The thing is, I have no idea what I want to be. You would think I'd want to be a Lego designer or something like that. The problem is that when someone tells me I *have* to do something, I wind up not wanting to do it. I'm worried that being a Lego designer would make me hate Legos, and that would be tragic. I figured I should choose a job that people would tell me I *shouldn't* do. I even made a list of those jobs:

1. Crocodile Wrestler

2. Fire Eater

3. Rattlesnake Tamer

But most of these jobs end in injury or death, and as you know, I am a giant coward. So I figured I should rethink things.

Boris's hand shot up.

"Yes, Big Chunks," Mr. K said.

"I'm going to go into the family business," he said.

Now this interested me, because I know nothing about Boris's family. I've never even seen them. The only thing I know about them is that his mother makes good spaghetti and his father likes to pretend that his green beans can talk to each other. I know this because Perry once had dinner at their house.

"What is your family's business?" Mr. K asked.

"They're worm farmers," said Boris.

Note to self: Never eat spaghetti at Boris's house.

LETHAL LUNCH

As it turned out, Boris's family doesn't actually *eat* the worms on their farm, which is called Red Wiggler Ranch. They sell the worms to people to use in compost bins. And once in a while people buy them to feed to their frogs.

Boris told the class that

the worms were called Red
Wigglers, and that they
have no ears and no eyes,
but they have five hearts.

"The better to love you
with," Boris said.

I wished he hadn't brought up
the whole worm farming thing, though,
because guess what they served for lunch
in the cafeteria? Spaghetti and tomato sauce!
It was impossible to eat it without thinking of
those Red Wigglers. Cat took my spaghetti and
gave me her box of raisins. But after I ate the
first one, I started thinking about Diablo's
raisins, so I couldn't eat those things either. I
just went straight to my dessert.

It was a bowl of rice pudding with a big blob
of whipped cream on it. I'll eat just about
anything if you put whipped cream on it.
Maybe even Red Wigglers. I stuck my spoon
into the bowl and suddenly . . .

SPLOOOOSH!!!!

The rice pudding exploded. Actually EXPLODED! It splattered all over me. There was rice pudding on my face, in my hair, and down the front of my shirt. To make matters worse, I screamed when it exploded. I have a very high-pitched scream. Okay, I'll just say it. I scream like a little girl on the teacup ride.

Everyone in the lunchroom was staring at me. But I ignored them because I was staring down at something else. Sitting in the middle of my rice pudding bowl was a Lego

Minifigure. It was a skeleton with an angry face, and he was holding something. I looked at it more closely. It looked like a turkey drumstick.

"Did you enjoy your rice pudding, Otis?" said a voice behind me.

I swung around and saw Sid Frackas. He was laughing. His tongue flopped all the way out of his mouth while he laughed and waggled around like a flounder.

"You!" I cried. "How did you *do* that?"

"Trade secret," Sid said.

"But how did you get it into my rice pudding?" I asked him.

"Let's just say I'm friends with the right people."

"You mean Flora the Lunch Lady?" I said.

"That's none of your business!" Sid's ears started turning red. "Look, if you know what's good for you, Otis Dooda, don't even THINK of entering that Lego contest. This time it was only rice pudding. Next time it will be something ten times worse."

That freaked me out. Being covered with rice pudding in the middle of the school lunchroom was already pretty bad.

Cat stood up and put her face so close to Sid's that their noses touched. "Bring it on, Frackas," she told him. "Otis isn't afraid of you."

I really wish she hadn't said that.

"Hey, Sid." Boris was holding up the Minifigure. "Why is this guy holding a turkey drumstick?"

"That's not a turkey drumstick," Sid said. "That's a club."

Cat looked at it again. "Nope. It's a turkey drumstick."

"It's a club!" Sid was getting really mad now.

"Let me see," said Cat, and took it from Boris.

"Yeah, Sid. It's definitely a turkey drumstick," she said. "A skeleton holding a turkey drumstick isn't scary, you know."

"Unless you're a turkey," said Boris.

Just then the cafeteria monitor came up to us and asked me why I had food all over me.

"The rice pudding exploded," I told her.

"Okay, Mr. Funny Man, come with me," she said.

I told her that I preferred Captain Mayhem, but she pretended not to hear me.

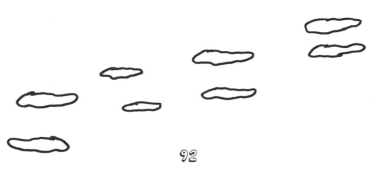

I'M A LI'L STINKER

They sent me to the nurse's office to get cleaned up. The nurse must have remembered my "scam" outburst about the germy hands, because she

didn't look happy to see me again. She looked even less happy when I told her that my rice pudding had exploded.

"Did you win Troublemaker of the Year award at your old school, Mr. Dooda?" she asked me.

"No," I said. "I won Most Amazing Lunch Box of the Year award," I said.

In fact, I got that award back in Hog's Head three years running.

After I took a shower in the back of her office, the nurse gave me a fresh shirt to put on for the rest of the day. The only problem was the shirt was for someone much, much smaller than me. It didn't even cover my belly button. Also it had a picture of a skunk on it and the words "I'm a Li'l Stinker."

I asked the nurse if she had any other shirts and she said she only kept clothes for kindergartners because they were usually the only ones who had "accidents."

I don't think she meant the kind of accident that involved rice pudding, either.

Unfortunately, gym was right after lunch. During jumping jacks I kept trying to yank the Li'l Stinker shirt down as far as it would go, but every time my arms went over my head, it pulled all the way up.

Myra kept staring at me. Then she started waving her hand at the gym teacher. "Miss Danvers, Miss Danvers! How come Otis gets to wear a sports bra to gym?"

Miss Danvers told her to keep jumping and mind her own business.

By the time we got back to our class, people were really snickering at my shirt. Mr. K took one look at me, pulled out his own nylon jacket

from the closet, and gave it to me to wear for the rest of the day.

I think he may be the nicest teacher I've ever heard of.

❄   ❄   ❄

After school, when Mom came to pick me up, she was walking Diablo *and* a new dog. It was a white greyhound with a cast on its front leg.

"Oh no," I groaned. "What's this one's problem?"

"He chased a car and broke his leg," Mom said.

"No, I mean what's his *problem*?" I said.

Every dog that is enrolled into Horrible Hounds Academy is seriously demented in some way.

"Oh, Archie is a sweetheart," Mom said happily. "He just needs a few basic obedience lessons. Why are you wearing that shirt, Otis?"

I didn't tell her about the rice pudding. She wouldn't have believed me anyway. I just told her I had an accident.

She looked at me, very concerned.

"You haven't had an accident since kindergarten. And how do you have an accident on your *shirt*? I've never even *heard* of someone having an accident on their shirt!"

Luckily a dog walked by just at that moment and Diablo went ballistic. Mom handed Archie's leash to me. Then she did her usual embarrassing thing where she rolled Diablo on his back, put her teeth on his throat, and growled.

That's when the *real* chaos happened!

It turned out that Archie did have

a problem: Whenever he got nervous, he whizzed.

The second Archie saw what was going on with Mom and Diablo, he started getting all jumpy. Then he lifted his leg to whiz. The only problem was that the cast on his front leg made him wobbly. While he was whizzing, he tottered and lurched and stumbled. He was spraying all over the place—on the window of a store, on some guy's shoes, and then on Mom. She jumped right up, and her shirt had a big whiz splotch on it.

"Now you've heard of *two* people who've had accidents on their shirts," I said to her, pointing at the splotch.

I got the Stink Eye for that one.

INVISIBILITY VESTS

After I finished my homework I headed over to Perry's apartment.

"Just in time, Otis!" Perry said when he opened the door. "Dad and I are going to test out some more of his party equipment. Want to help?"

Testing out Mr. Hooper's party equipment nearly always ends badly for me. In fact, like crocodile wrestling, it's the kind of thing most people would tell me NOT to do.

"Sure," I said. "What are we testing?"

"It's an Invisibility Vest," Mr. Hooper

explained as he pulled two puffy orange vests out of the BOY STUFF box.

"Come on, Mr. Hooper," I said. "You don't *really* think those vests will make us invisible, do you?"

"Put them on, boys!" Mr. Hooper said excitedly, handing us each a vest. "And there's more . . ."

He rummaged through the BOY STUFF box and pulled out two weird-looking hats. They were big square pieces of black metal with straps on them. After he strapped them onto

our heads, he attached some tubes and wires to the hats and the vests.

This was already starting to feel like a bad idea. I glanced over at Perry. He didn't look nervous at all.

Perry has total faith in his dad.

In all other ways, though, he is very intelligent.

"These hats are actually solar panels," Mr. Hooper said, "so we're going to have to go outside to try them."

"But, Mr. Hooper," I said as we headed toward the elevator, "how are we going to be invisible while wearing bright orange vests and solar panels on our heads? I think we'll be the opposite of invisible."

Mr. Hooper just smiled.

He stopped smiling, though, when he saw Julius the doorman in the lobby.

Julius looked us over with a grim expression on his face.

TRYING OUT A NEW GIZMO, MR. HOOPER? he said.

"Yes." Mr. Hooper looked scared.

"Make sure these boys come back with all their limbs intact, Mr. Hooper," said Julius.

"I will."

"And without their eyebrows missing from their faces," Julius warned.

Mr. Hooper hesitated.

That made me even more nervous.

Finally he said, "Sure thing, Julius."

As he hurried us outside, I caught a glimpse of Potted Plant Guy staring at us through the leaves. And laughing.

HEH, HEH, HEH.

When we were outside, Mr. Hooper said to us, "Question . . . what would you do if someone was shooting gum at you with the Bubble Blaster?"

"I'd run away," I said.

Perry said, "I'd do a front flip, then I'd karate chop the Bubble Blaster right out of his hands."

He would, too. Perry has some crazy ninja skills.

"Wrong!" Mr. Hooper cried. "You would use your Invisibility Vest!" He whipped out a piece of paper from his back pocket and started reading instructions out loud.

"'Flip on the switch in the front of the vest,'" he read.

Perry and I looked down at our vests, found the switches, and flipped them on.

"'Next, flap your arms like a chicken,'" Mr. Hooper read.

"Are you sure, Dad?" Perry said.

"That's what it says." Mr. Hooper waved the instructions at us.

Perry shrugged, then started flapping. I started flapping, too.

You would think people would stare at two kids who were wearing solar panels on their heads and flapping like chickens. But mostly people didn't pay much attention to us. At first, anyway.

After a minute or so something odd began to happen. Green smoke started to seep out of a tube in the back of our vests.

"Um, Dad. I think we're on fire," Perry said.

We did. But now it was looking like we *wouldn't* come back with our eyebrows still on our faces.

"Hey, Otis," Perry said. "Is it my imagination, or does this smoke smell bad?"

I took a sniff.

"Uggggh! It smells like clam chowder and body odor!"

The green smoke started getting thicker.
People were beginning to stare.

"Holy cow, what did you two eat for *lunch*?"
one guy said as he walked by, holding his nose.
"You're tooting green smoke!"

"That's a Texas Bean Bomber," a guy told
him. "I read about them in a medical book."

"Nah, that's a Thunder Dumpling," a lady said. "My grandfather used to do those after Sunday dinner."

"Don't stop flapping!" Mr. Hooper shouted. "Just think . . . if someone had a Bubble Blaster, they wouldn't be able to find you in all that smoke!"

More people were staring now. Most of them were laughing.

All I kept thinking was:

PLEASE DON'T LET SOMEONE I KNOW SEE ME.
PLEASE DON'T LET SOMEONE I KNOW SEE ME.
PLEASE DON'T LET SOMEONE I KNOW SEE ME.

Right about then, I spotted two of the Pony Tag girls from school walking up the street toward us.

"*Oh no*," I squeaked. I flapped my arms faster so that I could become "invisible" quicker. But when I saw the girls just a few yards away, staring at the green smoke, I panicked and started to run. The only problem was, I couldn't see where I was going with all that smoke.

I slammed into something. Luckily it was soft-ish. I think it might have been a lady. I'm pretty sure that she was fine, though, because I heard her say,

WHAT SMELLS LIKE DEAD POSSUM?

Finally all the street noise stopped, so I figured I was inside a building. Since I'd stopped flapping my arms, the smoke gradually began to clear. My eyes stung a little, so it took a minute to see where I was. You'll never believe it, but by some miracle I had made it back to the Tidwell Towers lobby and was standing right next to Julius.

I felt for my eyebrows. They were still there.

"Good news, Julius!" I said. "I still have all my limbs *and* my eyebrows!"

I knew he wasn't going to be too happy about me stinking up his lobby, so I wanted to keep things positive. But the look on Julius's face wasn't the look I was expecting. Instead of looking mad, he looked terrified.

"DON'T DO IT!!" he yelled.

"Don't do *what*?" I asked. But Julius wasn't looking at me. He was looking at Potted Plant Guy. "Oh no, oh no, oh no!" I cried when I realized what had happened. I hadn't seen where I was going with all that smoke, and I had passed Potted Plant Guy without putting something in his pail.

Potted Plant Guy's pinky and thumb were pointed directly at me. Between the leaves, his demented eyes were glinting.

He declared
his curse: "You will be
attacked by a swarm of angry bees!"

"Bees?!" I shrieked. "Not bees!"

Back in Hog's Head we had bees living in our
walls one summer. I found out because I
accidentally poked a hole in the wall with a fork

and I got
stung seven
times.

"Make it
something else,
Potted Plant Guy," I
begged. "How about
angry squirrels?"

To my amazement,
Potted Plant Guy actually
looked like he was considering
this.

Then he said: "Okay. Instead of
bees, you will be attacked by . . . a
swarm of angry yellow jackets."

"What?" I cried. "Yellow jackets are
even meaner than bees!"

But Potted Plant Guy had stopped pointing
at me. "The curse has been set. It cannot be
lifted!" he said.

I made a squeaking sound.

"Just remember, little man," Julius said,
"run in a zigzag pattern. It will confuse the
yellow jackets. Don't swat at them either.
And they like sweet smells."

He paused and made a face.

"I think you'll be fine in that
department," he said.

DIABOLICAL

After that, things went from horrible to extra horrible.

When I stepped into our apartment, Mom said, "You have a visitor, Otis. Hmm, what was his name . . . what *was* it . . . ?" Then she said in a whispery voice, "He has very big ears."

"Sid?" I asked, my voice already rising with panic.

"Sid! That's it," Mom said.

"Sid Frackas?! You let Sid Frackas in??"
I screamed.

"Calm down, mister," Mom said.

"Where is he? Is he . . . he's not?? . . . IS SID
FRACKAS IN MY ROOM??!!" I ran down the
hall and threw open the door to my room.

Sid had been standing on my desk, doing
something sneaky. I didn't know what it was
because he jumped down really fast and shoved
something in his pocket.

"So I see you decided to enter the contest," he said, gesturing to my hovercraft sketch and the printed-out copy of the Crazy Vehicle Lego Contest application form on the floor. "That was unwise."

"Did you do something in here?" I demanded.

"Are you still going to enter that contest?" he asked.

I guess I could have said no.

"Yes."

"Too bad," he said, as he backed out of my room. "If I can make rice pudding explode, just *imagine* what else I can do."

One of my problems is that I have an excellent imagination.

After he left, I searched the whole room for things that could possibly explode. I'll admit it, I was pretty freaked out. I was beginning to think that it would be a whole lot easier to forget all about the Lego contest.

That was when I heard a strange *ree-ree-ree* noise.

I followed the sound. It seemed to be coming from my dresser. Pressing my ear against each drawer I listened closely. The sound was definitely coming from my top drawer. My underwear drawer.

It might be a trap, I thought. I'd open the drawer and *KER-SPLAT!* Or *KA-SPLOOSH!* Or worse . . . *KA-BOOM!*

I put my hand on the drawer knob. The *ree-ree-ree* sound was getting even louder. I started to sweat. I considered just leaving the drawer closed. I could probably wear the underwear I had on for another week.

After a week, though, I'd have to wear Gunther's underwear.

That decided it. I'd just have to risk exploding myself.

I pulled the underwear drawer open very, very slowly. The *ree-ree-ree* noise suddenly stopped.

That was even creepier.

Okay, I said to myself. *You might as well just do it. Get it over with.* Squeezing my eyes shut, I yanked the drawer all the way open.

Nothing happened.

I opened my eyes.

There, sitting in the middle of my underwear, was Smoochie. He looked terrified. At least I think he looked terrified. It's hard to tell with a possibly brain-damaged rat.

"Sid locked you in there!? Aww, Smoochers! Poor little guy!" I picked him up and put him on my bed. He was shaking. That made me mad. Really mad. I'm not a big Smoochie fan, but being mean to a rat like Smoochie is just plain diabolical.

That settled it. I was going to enter that contest. Even if it killed me.

⚕ ÄLIËN ËGGS ⚕

The next day there was no school because of something called Teacher Development Day. Schools always have a bunch of these kinds of days. I've noticed that when the kids go back to school the next day, the teachers are always happier than usual. I am beginning to think that the teachers use these days to sit around and laugh at some of the dumb things we write in our homework. You know, to put

History
Homework

Where was the Declaration of Independence signed?

At the bottom.

themselves in a good mood for the rest of the week.

I worked on the hovercraft all morning. I had to admit, it was looking pretty good. I just had one little problem.

I needed a vacuum cleaner motor.

Luckily, we have a vacuum cleaner.

I snuck down the hall as quietly as possible. Mom was in the living room training Archie to sit. Excellent.

I opened the hallway closet where we keep the vacuum cleaner and started to pull it out when *RARF RARF RARF!* Diablo came charging at me.

That made Mom stop what she was doing to see what was going on. She took one look at me and the vacuum cleaner and she narrowed her eyes.

"What?" I said, trying to look insulted. "Is it a crime to want a tidy room?"

"It might be," she replied.

Luckily the doorbell rang just then. Quickly, I rolled the vacuum cleaner into my room while Mom tried to keep Diablo from mauling the person at the door.

It turned out to be Perry and Cat. They were all excited about something Miss Yabby had posted on the *Tidwell Tidbits*. They practically dragged me out of my room and into the thirty-fifth-floor hallway to see it.

So of course we rushed downstairs to touch the alien eggs.

When we got to the playground in the back of the building, there were a bunch of kids all crouching down by the pavement. Two kids from my class who also live in Tidwell Towers, Myra and Trevor McBride,

were there, too. Perry, Cat, and I crouched
down with them. Sitting in one of those little
paper ketchup cups that you get at McDonald's
were tiny yellowish eggs. Perry gave them a
poke, and then I did.

After a minute, Trevor said, "Hey, I think
one of them just moved!"

"Maybe they're hatching," another kid said.

We all watched for a few minutes. It was
actually pretty suspenseful. When nothing
happened, Perry said, "The thing is, if they're
aliens' eggs, what are they doing in a McDonald's
ketchup cup?"

That was when Trevor took one of the eggs out of the cup and ate it.

"TREVOR!!" everyone screamed. "THAT'S DISGUSTING!!"

"Now you're going to poop out an alien baby," Myra told him.

I don't think Trevor had thought things through very well, because he got really upset when he heard that. He started crying. I felt sort of bad for him, so I told him that they probably weren't alien eggs anyway.

"Yeah," Perry said,

THEY'RE PROBABLY JUST COCKROACH EGGS.

That made Trevor feel better.
Which is a little disturbing.

BZZZZZZ!

I spent the rest of the day tinkering with the hovercraft. I managed to get the motor out of the vacuum cleaner and installed in the hovercraft. I figured that once the contest was over, I could slip it back into the vacuum cleaner without Mom knowing.

Everything was going great . . . right up until I heard this weird metallic *bzzzzzzzing* noise coming from somewhere in my room. I wondered if it was something that Sid had hidden. After all, he did threaten that the next thing he did was going to be ten times worse than the rice pudding.

I walked around the room, listening carefully. It was weird but the sound seemed to be

moving. I just couldn't figure out where it was exactly. It was almost like it was in my walls.

Like the bees back in Hog's Head.

And then another thought occurred to me: That *bzzzzing* sounded an awful lot like a swarm of robotic bees.

Or robotic yellow jackets!

Boy, that really made me jittery. Because here's the thing about Potted Plant Guy's curses—they never happen the way you think they'll happen. I started imagining all those robotic yellow jackets swarming into the room and attacking me. Just the thought of that made me hyperventilate. But then I forced myself to calm down and think.

That's when I got a terrific idea.

Dogs have supersonic hearing. Maybe one of Mom's crackpot students could actually make himself useful.

"Hey, Mom," I said, "can I borrow Archie for a minute?"

I expected her to say no, but she said she had to walk Diablo and didn't feel like dealing with Archie's nervous whizzing problem again, so she said I was welcome to him.

"Okay, boy," I said to Archie once I got him in my room, "find the noise, find the noise!"

Archie got all excited. He started hopping all around my room, sniffing at everything. The only problem was that his leg with the cast on it stuck straight out and was smacking into all my stuff. He knocked a whole row of Lego *Star Wars* ships off my shelf and he swatted the garbage can to the ground. Then he jabbed me right in the thigh with that thing. But he really did seem to be onto something, so I let him keep hopping around. Finally, he stopped in front of my nightstand and barked at it.

"Here? Is it here?" I asked.

He barked again.

I'm telling you, the dog was some kind of genius.

I opened the drawer of the nightstand. The only thing in it was a comic book, some pencils, and a candy wrapper. But Archie kept staring at it with this wild look in his eyes.

Maybe it's behind the nightstand, I thought.

So I started moving the nightstand to look behind it. Archie got really excited then. That's when I knew I had found it! Ha! I was outsmarting Sid Frackas with a dog!

I moved the nightstand far enough away from the wall so that I could see what was back there. Sure enough, there was something balled up in the corner. It was gray and nasty looking. The *bzzzzzing* sound stopped.

Which was even creepier than the *bzzzzing.*

I took a pencil and poked at the thing lightly. It didn't explode. That was encouraging. So I stuck the pencil deeper into it and lifted it onto the top of the nightstand. Archie kept sniffing, then barking, then sniffing.

I sniffed, too.

It smelled familiar.

But familiar in a bad way.

I gathered up all my courage. I don't have a lot of courage, so it didn't take too long. I picked the thing up with my hands. Then I knew why it smelled familiar.

It was one of my old socks.

Filled with mayonnaise.

Archie's tail started wagging and he grabbed the sock in his mouth and hopped out of my room.

And of course, that's when the *bzzzzing* started up again.

So I did the only thing I could do. I fished out my Slinky from my closet and listened to the sound of *Star Wars* blasters until the *bzzzzing* stopped again.

AGENT SHAW

Trevor wasn't in school the next day. That got the kids from Tidwell Towers talking. Some of them said he was home sick with an alien egg in him. Myra said that the FBI was waiting outside his apartment to catch the alien baby when Trevor pooped it out.

I was beginning to feel really sorry for that alien baby.

"What's all this about aliens?" Boris asked.

"Didn't you see the alien eggs yesterday?" I asked him.

"Nah. I was doing my farm chores all day."

"Trevor might have eaten an alien egg," Cat told him.

Boris snorted. "That's ridiculous," he said.

"Probably," I agreed.

"Aliens don't lay eggs," he said. "They spit into a cup and put it in the fridge. Ten days later . . . *poof!* A baby alien is born."

"I don't think aliens have fridges, Boris," I said.

"Of course they do! Where else would they keep the leftover pizzas?"

❊　❊　❊

The day got even weirder if you can believe it. Right after attendance, Mr. K announced that we were having a special guest speaker to talk about his career. The classroom door opened and this guy walked in. He had on thick black-rimmed glasses and was dressed in a black suit. No one in the class seemed too excited, since he looked like a guy who fixed computers.

But then he said, "My name is Mr. Shaw and I am an agent for the FBI."

The kids from Tidwell Towers sort of gasped and looked at one another. Because this was a real coincidence.

"I know!" Mr. K said. "Cool, huh? Now everyone pay attention, because Mr. Shaw is going to give us an inside peek into the life of an FBI agent."

Mr. Shaw started talking about his training and a typical day for an agent. It was pretty interesting, especially the part about fingerprints and catching a thief who stole famous paintings from museums. But still, I think a bunch of us just kept thinking about Trevor.

After Mr. Shaw was done, he asked us if we had any questions. So of course every hand shot up in the air.

"Yes?" Mr. Shaw pointed to Myra.

"Are people from the FBI going to take Trevor McBride's alien baby?" she asked.

Mr. Shaw looked confused.

"Any *other* questions?" Mr. K said.

"If you did find an alien baby, what would you do with it?" another kid asked.

"Hmm, well." Mr. Shaw started looking uncomfortable. "I suppose we'd take it to a lab and examine it . . ."

"Yeah, but what if it flew around the room and you couldn't catch it?"

Mr. Shaw shuffled around. He folded his arms across his chest, then cleared his throat. He looked as if he wished he were back at work right now, chasing psychotic criminals.

"Okay, okay, gang!" Mr. K said. "Do you have any questions that are not about alien babies?"

I raised my hand.

"If you thought there was a dangerous robot or something hiding in your bedroom what would you do?"

Mr. Shaw sort of sighed. "Do you think you have a dangerous robot in your bedroom, young man?" he asked.

I got the feeling that Mr. Shaw was not going to volunteer to talk to any more classrooms for a long time. Also I was getting funny looks from Cat and Boris, which made me think I probably shouldn't mention the *bzzzzing* to them.

"Just in case I ever do," I said.

"Well, the other week we found a suspicious-looking package in a donut shop. We called in

the bomb squad and they shot a water cannon at it."

"You mean like a Super Soaker?" I asked.

"Something like that," he said.

I nodded, satisfied.

Because now I knew what I was going to buy with my $25.00.

ALIEN BABY INVASION

That afternoon I went out to buy my Super Soaker. When I got back to Tidwell Towers, I noticed a new *Tidwell Tidbits* by the elevator buttons. This one said:

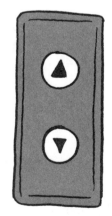

TIDWELL TIDBITS Jr.

After eating a Possible Alien Egg, Trevor McBride's condition is getting worse. The trouble is that no one knows if the alien egg he swallowed contains just one alien baby or 10,000 alien babies! I advise everyone to be on high alert, especially kids. Alien babies may have a tremendous appetite, and they will certainly look for bite-size humans.

Miss Yabby

I dropped off my Super Soaker at home. Then I went straight to Perry's apartment and told him about Miss Yabby's breaking news.

"I don't believe it about the alien babies," he said.

"Neither do I," I said.

We were quiet for a minute.

"But maybe we should have an Emergency Meeting anyway," Perry said.

"Right," I agreed.

We always hold our Emergency Meetings in Cat's bedroom, so we went across the hall to apartment 35F and rang the doorbell.

Cat's mom answered the door. She is just a little bigger than Cat and she doesn't speak English very well.

"You maybe looking for Cat Girl?" she said.

That made us giggle because Cat's mom named all her kids after comic strip characters. Cat's real name is Cat Girl.

"Yes, ma'am," said Perry.

"Hey." Cat's mom poked me in my chest. "How come Cat Girl not have any girl friends?" She seemed to think that was my fault somehow.

"Maybe because she's so scary?" I suggested.

"Mmm. Could be, could be." Cat's mom nodded. She let us in and we hurried down the hall to Cat's room.

Cat has the coolest room I've ever seen. It's probably the coolest room you've ever seen, too. It's a big wooden box that hangs in the air from chains attached to the ceiling. It looks like a gigantic cat condo, with holes cut out for windows, and carpet on the floor and walls.

Perry and I climbed up the rope ladder to get to her room and crawled in through one of the holes.

"We need to hold an Emergency Meeting," I said.

"Sssh!" Cat said.

She was sitting cross-legged on the floor.

"What are you—?" I started to ask her.

"SHHHHHHH!!!" she said. Then she looked all around the room suspiciously.

Perry and I looked all around, too. But the only thing we saw was Cat's room. We both shrugged at each other.

"All right," Cat said finally. "What's up?"

"The mother ship has landed," Perry announced.

"What?" she said.

"The hamster has lost his niblets," Perry said.

He always uses spy speak during Emergency Meetings. The problem is, no one ever knows what he's talking about.

Cat sighed. Then she looked at me for a
translation, so I told her about Miss
Yabby's newsletter.

I thought Cat would laugh at
us. But instead she got a
serious look on her face.

"Get me paper and a
pencil," she demanded.

I found a pencil and
notebook on her shelf and
brought it to her.

"Let's see," she said as she
started jotting down numbers.
"It takes about forty hours
for a sandwich to be digested.
You gotta figure an alien baby
might take a little longer than that."
She added a whole bunch of numbers, then
looked up at us. "According to my calculations,
Trevor will poop out the alien baby tomorrow
afternoon at approximately four thirty."

That was pretty impressive. I started to tell her so, but suddenly we heard "Ai-yi-yi-yi-yi-yi!!!!!"

The same face appeared in three different window holes. And each face was upside down. It was such a strange sight that I just sat there, shocked.

"Where did they come from?" Perry asked.

That's when I realized it was Cat's younger siblings, the triplets, Linus, Lucy, and Hobbes.

"I don't know," Cat said. "They've been hiding somewhere. They've been doing this all day." She jumped to her feet. "Run back and forth and slam into the walls!" she ordered.

We did. It made the whole room rock like mad.

"Ai-yi-yi . . . gaaaaaaaah!" cried Lucy. Then she disappeared and we heard a thump on the floor.

"Is she okay?" Perry asked.

"They bounce well," Cat said. "Keep running!"

"Ay-yi-yi-yi . . . eeeeeee!!" Linus dropped away, too.

Hobbes was hanging on pretty well though.
I began to feel sorry for him. Or her. To tell you
the truth I'm not sure what Hobbes is. So I
reached out and pulled Hobbes in.

Cat was not happy with me.
Hobbes, on the other hand,
jumped on my back,
wrapped his or her legs
around me, and
stayed there, like
a human backpack.

"So what do we do
about the alien baby?"
Perry asked Cat.

"We prepare
ourselves," Cat said.

"How?"

"Your dad has a whole box of BOY
STUFF he doesn't need until the weekend,
right?"

Perry nodded.

"So after school tomorrow, we let everyone have a Bubble Blaster or a Belly Button Popper and whatever else is in that box. That way, we'll be ready for an all-out alien invasion! Are you guys in?" She put out her fist for us to bump.

Perry bumped it.

Behind me, I felt Hobbes's head shaking NO! NO! NO!

And I kind of agreed. Putting Bubble Blasters in the hands of someone like Myra, for instance, just seemed to be asking for trouble.

Cat glared at me. "Well, Otis?"

I bumped her fist. Because, as you know, I am a big chicken.

I just hoped that alien baby was a real fast runner.

NOSTRIL TRICKS

The next day in school Cat passed this note to all the kids who lived in Tidwell Towers:

ALIEN BABIES will be invading today at 4:30.

BE PREPARED!

Rent your Anti-Alien Gear for 50¢. Rentals at apartment 35G at 4:15.

It did make me wonder if Cat really believed the alien babies would come, or if she just thought it was a good way to pick up a few bucks.

In any case, the kids loved the idea. In the lunchroom, there was a line of Tidwell Towers kids at our table handing us their milk money to rent Anti-Alien Gear, even Sid Frackas. After he paid his fifty cents, Sid bent down and whispered to me, "Hearing any mysterious sounds in your bedroom, Dooda?"

Then he laughed with that weird tongue-flapping thing he does and walked away.

So it wasn't my imagination! There was a *bzzzzzing* sound in my room!

I looked over at Sid. He had sat down at his table and was staring at me with this creepy grin on his face. It was very disturbing.

"Hey." Boris nudged me. "Want to see me stuff a tater tot up my nose?"

I figured anything would be better than watching Sid Frackas grinning at me.

Then I got a look at the tater tot. It was one of those super-jumbo kinds, about the size of a small kitten.

"There's no way that thing is going to fit up your nose," I said to Boris.

"Oh, you'd be surprised," Cat said. "I once saw Boris stuff a hard-boiled egg up his nose. His nostrils are very stretchy."

She wasn't kidding!

First, Boris did a little warm-up with his nose. He flared it a couple of times, then rubbed it and flared it again. It actually got bigger and bigger until . . . *SPLOOOOCH!* He shoved that tater tot straight up his left nostril!

"Wow! That's amazing!" I cried.

But he wasn't even done yet. In his right nostril he shoved a chicken nugget, a brussels sprout, and a cheese stick.

By the time he was finished, he had all five food groups up his nose.

"Okay, your turn," Boris said to me.

I looked down at my lunch tray. I had a turkey sub.

FOOD PYRAMID

"There's no way that's going to fit up my nose," I said.

"How about a baby carrot?" Cat suggested, handing me one from her plate.

"I don't know . . . ," I said. The thing is, my nostrils are skinny, like the rest of me.

"But it's a BABY carrot," Boris said. "It's not even a grown-up carrot."

I glanced over at Sid, who was still smirking at me. I don't know, I guess the pressure got to me. I took the baby carrot and shoved it up my nose. Sid suddenly quit smirking. Now he looked completely disgusted.

That's why I stuck a baby carrot up my other nostril, too. You know, to annoy him even more.

Then I started making seal noises. I wanted to make walrus noises, but

I wasn't sure what a walrus sounds like, so I settled for a seal.

For my big finish, I was going to blow those carrots out of my nose like two missiles. I figured that would really ruin Sid's lunch. I took a big, long, deep breath, then . . .

Shluuuurp!

Uh-oh.

I must have had a funny look on my face because Cat said, "Did you suck those baby carrots farther up your nose?"

I nodded.

"Do you need the nurse?" she asked.

I nodded.

Then sighed.

Because that woman was not going to be happy to see me.

FACE-HOLES

The thing you should know about baby carrots is that they go up your nose a lot easier than they go back down your nose.

After I told the nurse what had happened, she said, "What face-hole are you supposed to put your food into, Mr. Dooda?"

"My mouth," I said glumly.

Actually, I said, "By bowth," because another thing you should know is that you sound funny with baby carrots up your nose.

"Correct, Mr. Dooda." She said it just like I was about three and a half years old. "From now on let's put the right things in the right face-holes, okay?"

Then she muttered something about counting down the days until her trip to Bermuda.

She tried to get me to blow the carrots out of my nose, but those little suckers were wedged in there tight. After that, she tried to get them out with tweezers. No luck.

In the end, she called my mom and told her she had to take me to the doctor.

Mom was even less happy to see me than the nurse was. When I asked her

if we were going to the doctor, she said she wasn't going to wait in an emergency room for the next six hours. She said she was going to take matters into her own hands.

"Maybe we can just leave the carrots where they are," I suggested nervously.

"Those carrots are coming out of that nose one way or another, buster," she said.

I didn't like the sound of that.

MIGHTY MACK 500

To my horror, the first thing Mom did when we got home was march to the closet and pull out the vacuum cleaner.

"What are you going to do with that?" I asked.

"Don't worry," she said.

But I was worried. Not about my nose. I was worried because the

vacuum cleaner's motor was currently sitting in my hovercraft.

Of course when Mom flipped the vacuum cleaner switch, nothing happened. She flipped it a couple more times while I tried to look innocent.

"Darn old thing!" she said.

I shook my head in disgust at the vacuum cleaner.

I was just congratulating myself for getting off so easily, when Mom said, "All right, we're going downstairs to see Julius."

That made me nervous all over again. I like Julius, but he is kind of scary, too. I wondered if Mom was going to have him flip

me upside down and shake the carrots out of me. It turned out, though, that she only wanted Julius to get her the lobby's vacuum cleaner.

"It's to suck the carrots out of Otis's nose," Mom told Julius.

Julius looked at me for a long time. Then he said, "Don't you know which face-hole to stick your food into, son?"

"I do dow, Juliuth," I mumbled.

Julius rolled out the lobby vacuum cleaner, which looked like a jet engine on wheels. It was something called the Mighty Mack 500, and Julius said it could suck the skin off a lemon.

"Maybe this isn't such a good idea," I said.

"I know what I'm doing," Mom insisted. "I once removed a candy cane from your brother's nose this way." Then she got red in the face, like she hadn't meant to say that.

"Is that why he never picks his nose anymore?" I cried. "Because you used a vacuum cleaner to suck a candy cane out of his nose? Listen, lady, that's not going to happen to me—"

But before I could finish, she flipped the switch on the Mighty Mack 500 and stuck the nozzle against my nose.

BROARRRRRRRRRRR!!!!!!

The thing not only looked like a jet engine, but it sounded like one, too. And boy oh boy, was it powerful! I felt the carrot in my left nostril begin to vibrate. If the nozzle had been any bigger, I'm pretty sure my whole body would have been sucked right into the hose.

Within a few minutes a crowd had begun to form around me in the lobby. I guess most people have never seen a person with a vacuum cleaner up their nose before. They seemed like they were really enjoying themselves, too.

I BET HE STUCK A PENNY UP HIS NOSE,

one lady said.

"From the size of that vacuum, he must have stuck an entire cash register up his schnozz," a guy said.

"Wow," said someone else, "it looks like that thing is going to suck his brains right out of his head!"

Now that really worried me. In fact, the very next second I really did begin to feel like my brain was getting tugged through my nose. Everything got really tight in there and I felt this pressure building and building . . .

CLAP CLAP CLAP CLAP

"Turn off the Mighty Mack!" I cried out. "It's sucking out my brains!"

But between the roar of the vacuum and the carrots up my nose, no one understood what I was saying. Right then I felt something shoot out of both nostrils and clatter around in the vacuum hose.

"Oh no, *my brains, my brains!*" I cried.

Mom shut off the Mighty Mack 500. She looked up my nose. Then she smiled.

THE CARROTS ARE GONE! she declared,

and everyone in the crowd applauded.

I guess I should have been happy. The carrots were out of my nose, and my brains were still in my head.

But now there were two things I knew for sure:

1. Miss Yabby was going to hear about this.
2. I was never, ever going to put anything up my nose again. Not even my finger.

MY DISGUSTING FAMILY

After that traumatic event I planned to spend the rest of the day relaxing on the couch. Mom had other plans for me, though. Apparently getting baby carrots stuck up your nose doesn't count as a sick day.

Mom's plan was to pick up a whole bunch of creams:

1. ZIT CREAM FOR GUNTHER,

2. FOOT FUNGUS CREAM FOR MOM,

3. HEMORRHOID CREAM FOR DAD.

SCRATCH SCRATCH

In other words, my whole family is totally disgusting.

(In case you don't know what hemorrhoid cream is, I'll just say that it has to do with an itchy heinie. I didn't know my father had this problem, but it does explain why he gets so cranky on long car rides.)

To make matters worse, Mom took Archie and Diablo along to buy this stuff. Every time Diablo tried to attack another dog, Archie began to stagger around, whizzing all over the place. We had to dodge the whiz each time. Plus Mom couldn't bite Diablo's neck unless she wanted to get whizzed on.

When we got to the drugstore, Mom told me to hold on to the dogs while she went inside.

"No way," I told her. "You can't leave me alone with these maniacs."

"Fine," she said, and handed me a twenty-dollar bill. "You go in and buy the stuff."

That seemed like a better deal. I went into the drugstore, found all the items on the shelf, and brought them to the cashier. She smiled at me.

"No school today?" she said.

"Oh, I just, um . . . had a few medical issues," I told her. I figured that was less embarrassing than explaining about the baby carrots.

After she rang up the zit cream and the foot fungus cream, she gave me this sad look. But when she picked up the hemorrhoid cream she looked like she was about to cry.

That's when I realized she thought they were all for me! I was just about to tell her that they were for my disgusting family and I was the only normal one, when she pulled out a box of lollipops from under the counter.

"Go on. Help yourself, you poor little guy."

Well, I can't resist a freebie, so I took three of them.

But I scratched my heinie on my way out, just to make her feel like she had done a good deed.

2 WEIRD 4 GUNTHER

The last disgusting item we needed to pick up was Pandora.

There was no school in Hog's Head that day, so she was taking the bus to New York City. It dropped her off close by, so we strolled over to the bus stop to meet her. On the way, Diablo tried to attack no less than fourteen

dogs while Archie sprayed everyone in the vicinity.

"I'm beginning to think that Diablo is a hopeless case," Mom said finally.

I started worrying about his raisins all over again.

The bus had just pulled in when we arrived at the stop. We watched as people got off the bus, but no Pandora.

"Maybe she decided not to come," Mom murmured.

The way she said that made me wonder if she was *hoping* Pandora wasn't on that bus. She

doesn't think Pandora is a good girlfriend for Gunther. I know this because I read a text message that she wrote to Dad.

Finally, we caught sight of Pandora stepping off the bus. It was hard to miss her actually, because she had dyed her hair bright green. Plus she was wearing a silver cape. That's right, a cape.

She said a word that I can't put in this book.

Just at that moment a dog walked by and Diablo started going crazy as usual. I guess Mom was too surprised to keep Archie from whizzing all over the place. Instead, Archie just whizzed right on Diablo's head. And guess what? That devil dog was so shocked, he stopped barking on the spot! The whole way home, Diablo was quiet as a mouse.

I hoped that meant he could keep his raisins after all, because this whole raisin thing was giving me the jim-jams.

ROBOT YELLOW JACKETS

By the time we got back home, Gunther was there. When he and Pandora saw each other, they were so happy they started picking and scratching at themselves like crazy. You won't believe this, but Gunther didn't even seem to *notice* that Pandora's hair was green. I guess if you don't notice that your girlfriend looks like

a leprechaun it must mean that you really are in love.

Mom announced that Pandora was going to share my room, and I had to help her get settled in. I wasn't too thrilled about that plan, let me tell you. Pandora followed me into my room and plopped her bags down on my bed. The very next second, the *bzzzzing* started.

"Did you know there are robot yellow jackets in your wall?" Pandora said.

I could have hugged her for that!

So I told her about Sid Frackas. She listened very carefully while she scratched at her green head. Every so often she frowned and nodded. I started to think that maybe I had misjudged Pandora all this time.

When I was done, there was a long pause.

Then she said, "Do you think Gunther liked my hair?"

Seriously. That's what she said.

The *bzzzzing* was getting louder. Now it sounded like the swarm of robotic yellow jackets had tripled.

"Pandora," I said, "listen carefully."

She immediately started scratching her head. "And stop scratching your head," I told her. And you know what? The second she stopped scratching her head, she got this very alert look in her eyes. I think all that scratching makes her brains vibrate too much.

"Take this"—I handed her the hovercraft— "and run—"

Before I could finish telling her to run to the living room with it, she grabbed the hovercraft and bolted out the door. I heard Gunther call

out, "Pandora? Pandora! Where are you going?"
And then the front door slammed shut.

Never mind, I thought. *It's okay as long as Pandora keeps the hovercraft safe from Sid.*

I grabbed my Super Soaker out from under my bed. The minute those robot yellow jackets burst through my walls, I'd be ready for them.

Suddenly the *bzzzzzzing* sound stopped. The very next second there was a new noise.

Something was banging against my wall, trying to get in.

My heart was drumming against my chest like mad. I also might have been making that hee-hee-hee sound again.

Then . . . *KUNK! BLAM!*

Something came shooting right out of the air vent in my wall and landed on my

bed. It happened so fast I didn't even have time
to aim my Super Soaker. I just stared and blinked.

Because this was NOT what I expected.

"Linus, Lucy, Hobbes," I said, staring down
at the three of them piled up on my bed. "What
the heck are you doing?"

Hobbes put a finger
behind each ear and
pushed them forward
so that they stuck out.

"Sid Frackas put you up to this?" I asked.

All three nodded.

"What did he want you to do?"

Linus took a hammer out of his back pocket. He pointed to my hovercraft sketch and pretended to *whack, whack, whack* it with the hammer.

"Awww, man." I shook my head at them in disappointment. "I thought you guys were my friends."

The triplets all looked ashamed of themselves.

"So what did he give you to do this?" I asked. "Money?"

They shook their heads.

Hobbs pulled out a lollipop from his pocket and held it up. He pushed a button on the stick and the lollipop started spinning.

"You did it for a spinning lollipop?"

He nodded his head.

Then Lucy and Linus took their motorized lollipops out of their pockets and started spinning them, too.

Here's an interesting fun fact:

Spinning lollipops sound an awful lot like robot yellow jackets.

BZZZZZZZZZZ

THE ANTI-ALIEN PATROL

Once I shooed Linus, Lucy, and Hobbes back to their apartment, I went to look for Pandora.

Luckily, green-headed people are easy to spot.

"Yeah, I saw her," Julius said. "She ran right out the lobby door just a few minutes ago. She was headed in the direction of the playground."

"Thanks!" I said and ran toward the door, too. Behind me I could hear a rustle of plant leaves and the sound of Potted Plant Guy laughing.

"Heh, heh, heh."

Pandora was in the playground. Well, not exactly *in* the playground. She was about a foot above the playground. Riding on my hovercraft!

"Hey!!" She waved to me as she zoomed by. "Did you know this thing flies?"

It was flying really well, too. She zipped around the monkey bars and leaned to the left to make it swoop back toward me. I have to admit it . . . she could ride that thing like a pro.

I had a big smile on my face. Because now I was pretty sure that my hovercraft could win the

contest. I didn't know what Sid's entry was going to be, but I doubted it would be anywhere near as cool as what I had built.

As soon as I thought that, guess who comes walking into the playground?

That's right.

Sid Frackas.

"HA!" I said to Sid. "Looks like you wasted your money on those spinning lollipops. My hovercraft is alive and

well"—Pandora did a figure eight—"and totally awesome."

"How disappointing for me," Sid said while watching Pandora on the hovercraft.

But he didn't look disappointed. That should have been a tip-off, but I was just so excited about my hovercraft, I didn't think about it. Suddenly, Sid whipped a walkie-talkie out of his pocket, turned around, and whispered something into it.

In a matter of seconds, about a dozen Tidwell Towers kids came rushing into the playground, including Cat, Perry, and Boris. The strange thing was, they were all wearing yellow raincoats. On the back of the raincoats the words "Bubble Blaster Jackets" was crossed off in magic marker. In its place someone had written ANTI-ALIEN PATROL on each jacket.

"What did you do, Sid Frackas?" I demanded.

"I just sealed your doom," he said coolly.

"There it is!!!" Boris shouted. He was pointing at my hovercraft.

"LET'S GO GET IT!!" shouted Cat, and held up a bow and arrow.

"No! Wait!" I yelled. "That's for the Lego contest!"

"Who cares about a Lego contest!" Myra said. "We're trying to get the alien on that flying saucer!"

I looked at Pandora. And her crazy green hair. And her silver cape. Floating a foot off the ground.

Uh-oh.

WAR OF THE WORLDS

The Anti-Alien Patrol all rushed toward Pandora and the hovercraft.

Cat was holding her bow and arrow with the water balloon on the tip. She took aim, pulled her arm back, and the arrow went soaring through the air, straight for the back of Pandora's head. Pandora ducked just in the nick of time, and the arrow hit the playground slide. Only it wasn't water that was in the balloon. It was some yellow-brownish stuff. I didn't even want to think about what *that* was.

Then Myra used the Toilet Paper Launcher, and a roll of toilet paper shot into the air. It started unwinding all over the place and dropped down directly over Pandora. She banked the hovercraft to the right to avoid it and started weaving between the swings.

Go, Pandora!

Just then I noticed that a couple of kids on the Anti-Alien Patrol had shoved something in their mouths and were chewing like mad.

Bubble Blasters! A few good hits from one of those things, and my hovercraft would be toast! "STOP!" I screamed.

Just when it seemed like it couldn't get any worse, I spotted Boris rubbing something between his hands. Then he picked up his shirt and put it in his belly button and pointed his belly at Pandora.

Oh no! He had preheated a Belly Button Popper!

I heard the *tssssss* sound and the popper, covered with Boris's belly-button hair, came shooting at Pandora. I ran toward her, waving my arms.

"Duck, duck!" I shouted. But when I turned around I saw that the popper was now headed directly for me! I was paralyzed with fear as I

watched the furry missile coming closer, closer, CLOSER—

Then, *woooooosh*—there was a rush of air as Pandora swooped in beside me. Grabbing me by my waist, she pulled me onto the hovercraft a second before the popper would have clocked me in the head and off we sped.

"Look!" Boris screamed. "The alien has Otis! That thing

will
take him
back to the
mother ship and do
weird experiments on him!"

"Come on, guys, we have to save
him!" Perry shouted.

"It's okay, everyone!" I cried out to them. "It's
just Pan—" but before I could finish, Cat had let

one of her arrows fly. It hit me on my shoulder and the yellow-brownish gunk splattered all over me and Pandora.

To my horror, Pandora licked it off her arm.

"Yummers, honey-mustard dressing," she said.

"Sorry, Otis!" Cat screamed.

I glanced backward. The entire Anti-Alien Patrol was charging at us, their yellow jackets flapping like mad.

Yellow jackets.

Then I remembered Potted Plant Guy's curse:
*You will be attacked by a swarm of angry
yellow jackets.*

"Pandora!" I cried. "Put the hovercraft on
Deep-Pile Carpet speed!"

I grabbed Pandora around her waist and she
hit the switch.

The hovercraft lurched forward so
fast we both almost toppled
backward. Then it took off.
Man, that hovercraft
was cooking! We were
whipping across the
playground at
top speed.
Cat's
arrows
were
splattering
all around
us and

the sky was filled with unraveling toilet paper rolls.

Up ahead I could see some of the kids stuffing gum into their Bubble Blasters.

"Quick, Pandora," I cried, "head for the log tunnel!"

Pandora swerved around and aimed for the opening of the tunnel made to look like a long wooden log. It would be a tight fit. An inch to the right or the left and we wouldn't make it. But Pandora had really good aim. We zipped right into the tunnel no problem, just as the Bubble Blasters started

shooting bubble gum at us. We could hear the gum hitting against the outside of the tunnel. *Ping!! Ping-ping! Ping-ping! Ping-ping-ping-ping!*

Then it got quiet. They must be out of gum, I thought. They'd be chewing those gum bricks right about now, ready to reload. If we hurried, we could zoom right out of the playground and be safe and sound back in Tidwell Towers. Julius would make everyone drop their anti-alien gear. And I would defeat Sid Frackas.

That was the plan, anyway.

Unfortunately Boris was waiting at the other end of the tunnel. And he was aiming his belly button right at us.

The force of that hairball knocked Pandora and me right off the hovercraft. We landed in a pile by the sand pit. The hovercraft flew a few feet more before getting tangled in the swings.

That's when Sid saw his chance.

"Smash the flying saucer so the alien can't escape again!" he cried.

The Anti-Alien Patrol rushed in and surrounded the hovercraft. Before I could stop it, I heard the sound of Legos crashing and then the *stomp, stomp, stomp* of sneakers on a vacuum cleaner motor.

GIANT BUMMER

"Aww, I'm sorry, Otis," Perry said after everything settled down and I explained that Pandora was Gunther's girlfriend, and the hovercraft was my Lego contest entry.

"We were just trying to protect you," Cat said. She even put her arm around me. Usually when she does that, something bad happens next. But this time, she just patted my shoulder.

Myra was still suspicious, though. She turned to Pandora and asked point-blank, "Did Trevor poop you out?"

"Who's Trevor?" Pandora asked.

Which seemed like a weird response, if you think about it.

"Trevor is the guy who ate one of the little yellow alien eggs in the ketchup container," Myra said.

"Yellow eggs?" Boris said. "In a ketchup container? No one told me the eggs were yellow and in a ketchup container."

"Does that matter?" I asked him.

"Well, yeah. Because those weren't alien eggs," Boris said. "They were Red Wiggler worm eggs."

"Worm eggs!" Cat cried. "What were worm eggs doing in a ketchup container in the playground?"

"I was giving them some fresh air," Boris said.

"Then my hovercraft was busted up because of WORM EGGS?" I cried.

"Looks that way, doesn't it?" Sid Frackas said. "Listen, Dooda, Tidwell Towers is only big enough for one Lego genius, and you're looking at him." Then he started laughing. His tongue flopped all the way out of his mouth and waggled around.

"Hey, what are those bumpy things on your tongue, Sid?" Cat asked.

We all looked at his tongue. There were these little red blisters all over it. Sid yanked that flounder-tongue right back into his mouth. "Anyway, get ready to congratulate me on winning first prize in the Lego contest, Dooda. You won't be able to fix that thing by tomorrow."

I looked at the messed-up hovercraft and the smashed vacuum-cleaner motor.

He was right. Even if I could rebuild the Legos, there was no way I'd be able to find another vacuum-cleaner motor in time.

I was so bummed about my hovercraft that I had no appetite for dinner. No one else was eating much, either. Gunther and Pandora were too busy making goo-goo eyes at each other.

And Mom and Dad were too busy text-messaging each other about Gunther and Pandora. Even Smoochie didn't seem very hungry.

I couldn't sleep that night, either, and not just because I was lying on the floor in a sleeping bag while Pandora was scratching her scalp in my bed.

"Are you sad about your hovercraft?" Pandora said.

"Yeah."

"Want to see me do shadow puppets with my toes?" she asked.

"Kind of," I said.

So she did the entire

Charlie Brown Christmas Special with her toes.
It was really good, too. Her big toe looked
exactly like Charlie Brown's head.

Pandora may not be so bad after all.

DINGLE-DORK OF THE WEEK →

he next day, right after lunch, the doorbell rang. Mom answered it, and Cat, Boris, and Perry burst in, all looking very happy.

"You won, Otis!" Perry said.

"That's impossible," I told them. "I never even entered the Lego contest."

"Not *that* contest," Perry said. He handed me a piece of paper. "Go on. Read it."

I read out loud:

Special Alien Baby Update
Good news! There will be no alien baby invasion.

Trevor's mother says, "Trevor is NOT sick because of an alien baby, and will everyone please stop saying that? He is sick with foot and mouth disease."

Probably because anything stuck to the bottom of his foot goes directly into his mouth. By the way, foot and mouth disease is very contagious.

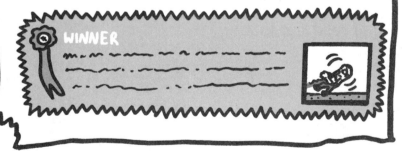

WINNER

"Look what it says below." Perry pointed to the next item.

WINNER

Winner of the Dingle-Dork
of the Week Award
Otis Dooda, apt 35B
Otis gave us all a giggle
when he decided to feed his
nose some baby carrots.
Congratulations, Otis! You win a giant-size
Tootsie Roll and a new vacuum cleaner, in case
you decide to feed your nose the giant-size
Tootsie Roll.
Please see Julius to claim your prize.

1st PLACE

"A new vacuum cleaner!" Mom cried.

I'm not going to lie to you. For a half second
I considered taking apart the new vacuum
cleaner and rebuilding the hovercraft.

But Mom looked so happy about the vacuum
cleaner. And even though winning the Dingle-Dork
of the Week award wasn't nearly as good as
winning first prize in the Lego contest, it was

better than Most Amazing Lunch Box of the Year award.

Plus, I really like Tootsie Rolls.

❉   ❉   ❉

So it all turned out okay in the end. True, I didn't win $500 and Lego fame and glory. But neither did Sid. He didn't even get a chance to enter the Lego contest. It turned out those blisters on his tongue were from foot and mouth disease. He spent the whole next week sick in bed.

HERE'S THE LEGO VEHICLE THAT DID WIN:

HI, MOM!

Pretty cool, huh? It gave me an idea for my next Lego invention. I'm not going to tell you about it just yet, though. I might jinx it. Maybe you don't believe in jinxes, but trust me, they're real. Since I've moved to Tidwell Towers I've learned that anything can happen.

THE END

HANG ON A SECOND...
THE FUN'S NOT OVER!

HEAD OVER TO
OTISDOODA.COM

You'll find **ACTIVITIES** to do at home or school!

OTIS' BEST BUILDERS BLOG,

where you can show off your own brick creations
and get a comment from Otis!

You can also keep up with **OTIS & CAT** by following their **TWITTER** feeds!

latest tweets

Otis Dooda 12 Sep
@OtisDooda

Are you a LEGO fan? COOL CREATIONS IN 35 PIECES by @seankenney! ow.ly/oDJs0

Cat Catalano 9 Jul
@CatGirlCatalano

Who IS Mr. Tasty?!? This TV show is better than ANYTHING on the air right now!!! Polaris rules...

youtube.com/watch?v=J7lGup...

▶ Show Media

ALL OF THIS AND MORE AT

OTISDOODA.COM

HEY! DID YOU KNOW THIS BOOK HAS A SOUNDTRACK? ♫ ♪

All songs written and performed by David Heatley.
Produced by Sanford Livingston.

FEATURING the soon-to-be-smash-hit song
"THE GREATEST LEGO GENIUS THAT EVER LIVED"

THAT'S ME! AND DON'T YOU FORGET IT!!!

Check out what some kids' music experts said about the soundtrack to the first Otis book, *Strange But True!*

"ENGROSSING SONGS . . . VIVID CHARACTERS."—Jeff Bogle, *Out With the Kids*

"RAD, RAD, RAD."—Eva Glettner, *Babble*

"STELLAR MUSICIANSHIP."—Mindy Thomas, Program Director of *Sirius/XM's Kids Place Live*

"[AN] IMAGINATIVE COLLECTION OF OFFBEAT FAMILY SONGS."—Kathy O'Connell, host and producer *Kids Corner*, WXPN

ABOUT ELLEN POTTER

I grew up in NYC, where I lived in an apartment building nearly as weird as Tidwell Towers. I've written ten books, including *THE HUMMING ROOM, THE KNEEBONE BOY, OLIVIA KIDNEY,* and *SLOB*. Although I've never owned a farting horse, I do have a bull terrier who beeps his horn pretty regularly. I live in Maine and am still waiting to see a moose.

To get in touch with me and learn more about my other books, visit ELLENPOTTER.COM.

ABOUT DAVID HEATLEY

David drew all the pictures for this book, in addition to writing the songs for both Otis books' soundtracks. When he's not playing with Legos or daydreaming, he creates art for magazines, books, and Web sites all over the world, including *THE NEW YORKER*, *THE NEW YORK TIMES*, and *NICKELODEON*. He lives in the same city as Otis, but his neighbors aren't nearly as crazy.

Drop him a line at **DAVIDHEATLEY.COM**.

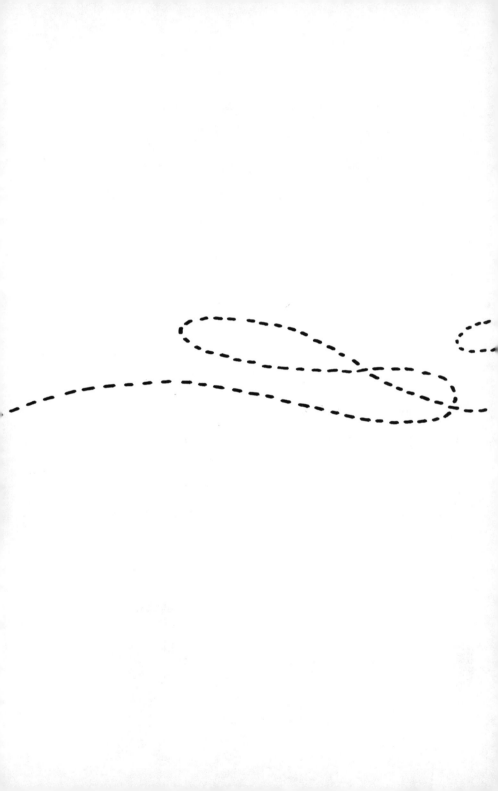

Thank you for reading
this FEIWEL AND FRIENDS book.
The Friends who made

OTIS DOODA
DOWNRIGHT DANGEROUS

possible are:

JEAN FEIWEL, *Publisher*

LIZ SZABLA, *Editor in Chief*

RICH DEAS, *Senior Creative Director*

HOLLY WEST, *Associate Editor*

DAVE BARRETT, *Executive Managing Editor*

NICOLE LIEBOWITZ MOULAISON, *Production Manager*

LAUREN A. BURNIAC, *Editor*

ANNA ROBERTO, *Assistant Editor*

Follow us on Facebook or visit us online at mackids.com.

OUR BOOKS ARE FRIENDS FOR LIFE.